The Happy Heart Princess

LEONIE JADE NORTON

Illustrated by: Shannen Marie Paradero

AuthorHouse™ UK
1663 Liberty Drive
Bloomington, IN 47403 USA
www.authorhouse.co.uk
Phone: 0800 047 8203 (Domestic TFN)
+44 1908 723714 (International)

Because of the dynamic nature of the Internet, any web addresses or links contained in this book may have changed
since publication and may no longer be valid. The views expressed in this work are solely those of the author and do not
necessarily reflect the views of the publisher, and the publisher hereby disclaims any responsibility for them.

Any people depicted in stock imagery provided by Getty Images are models,
and such images are being used for illustrative purposes only.
Certain stock imagery © Getty Images.

This book is printed on acid-free paper.

ISBN: 978-1-7283-9728-3 (sc)
ISBN: 978-1-7283-9727-6 (e)

Print information available on the last page.

Published by AuthorHouse 01/15/2020

authorHOUSE®

The Happy Heart Princess

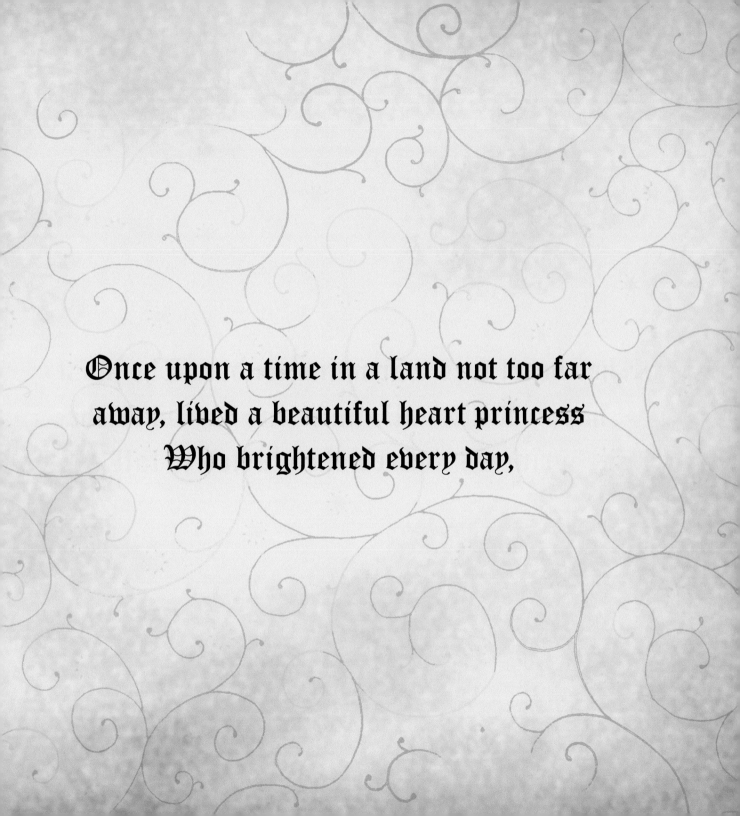

Once upon a time in a land not too far away, lived a beautiful heart princess Who brightened every day,

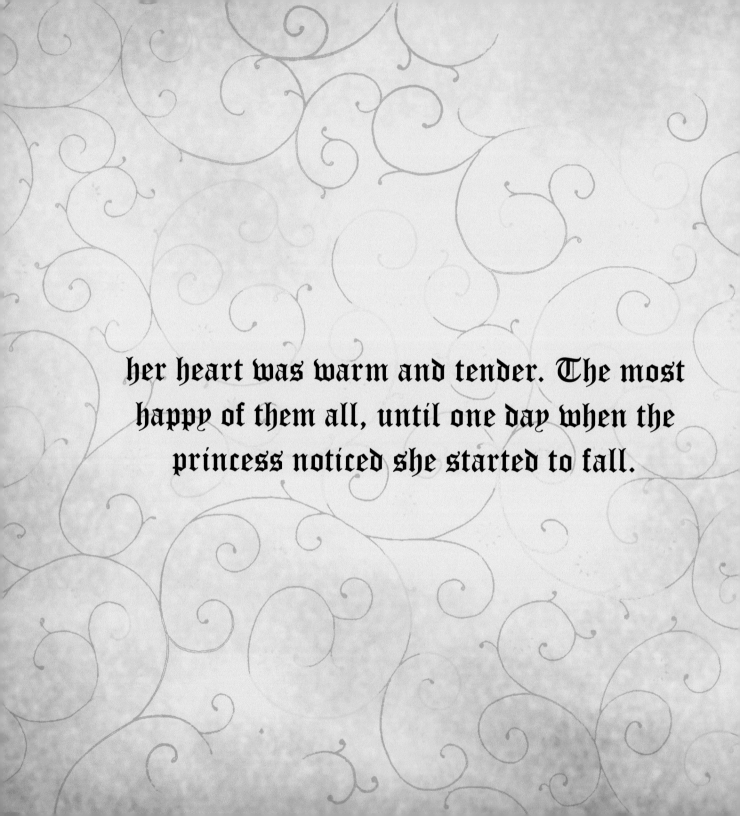

her heart was warm and tender. The most happy of them all, until one day when the princess noticed she started to fall.

Fall down, not too badly and did so in a positive way. Because how could such a happy princess, have that a bad day?

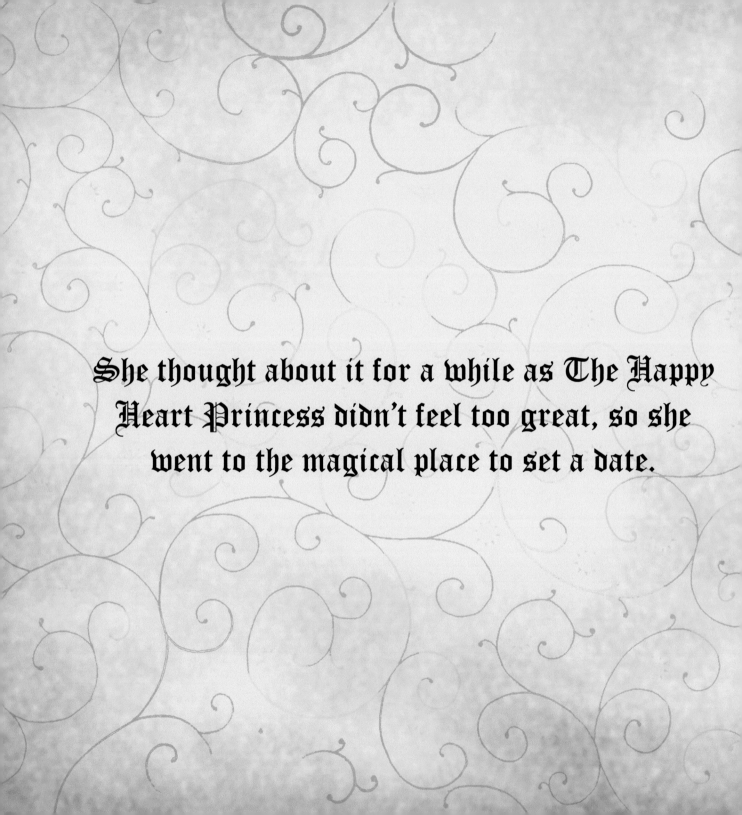

She thought about it for a while as The Happy Heart Princess didn't feel too great, so she went to the magical place to set a date.

The fairies looked at her closely & checked she was ok. Because how could The Happy Heart Princess be feeling that way.

The magical fairies bought The
Heart Princess close- I'm sorry my
dear it's what we feared most.
Your happy heart my princess is not
how it's supposed to be, and we will
need to treat it very carefully.

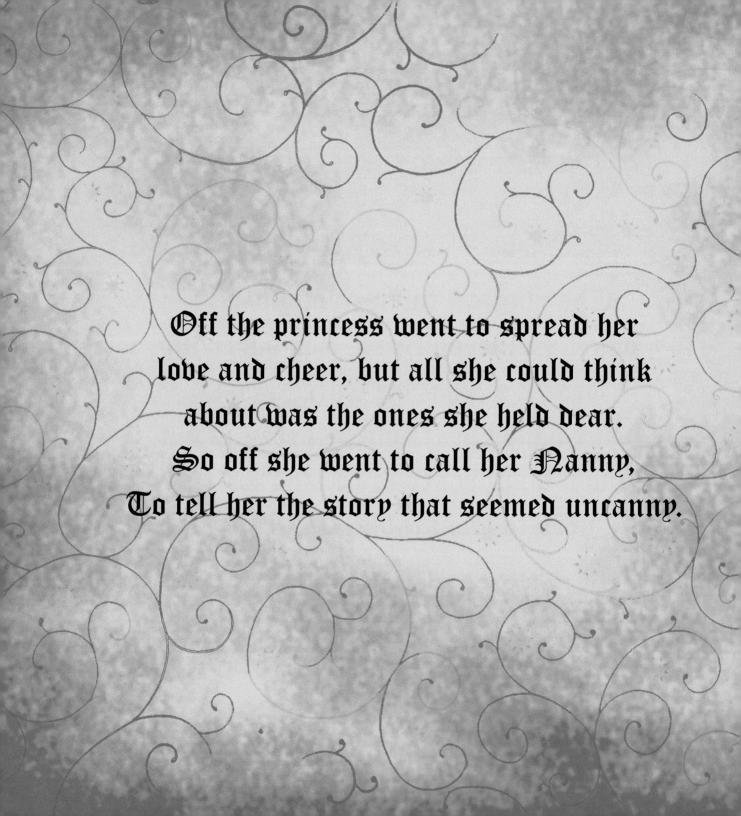

Off the princess went to spread her
love and cheer, but all she could think
about was the ones she held dear.
So off she went to call her Nanny,
To tell her the story that seemed uncanny.

Nanny N Nanny N how can it be that
my heart does not work perfectly?
Well my dear I'll have you know they
pick the best ones to help them grow.

But Nanny N Nanny N what If I don't
want this, why does it have to be me?
Well my darling don't you see.
You have a happy heart that is made to be loved.
And then to help those from around and above.

Don't be afraid, don't you see
the love you have it's so clear to me.
We only have things to help us shine
and my dear this is your time.

Show them fairies what your made of and
that you were a gift sent from above.
Fill hearts with hope and happiness
you have so much love.

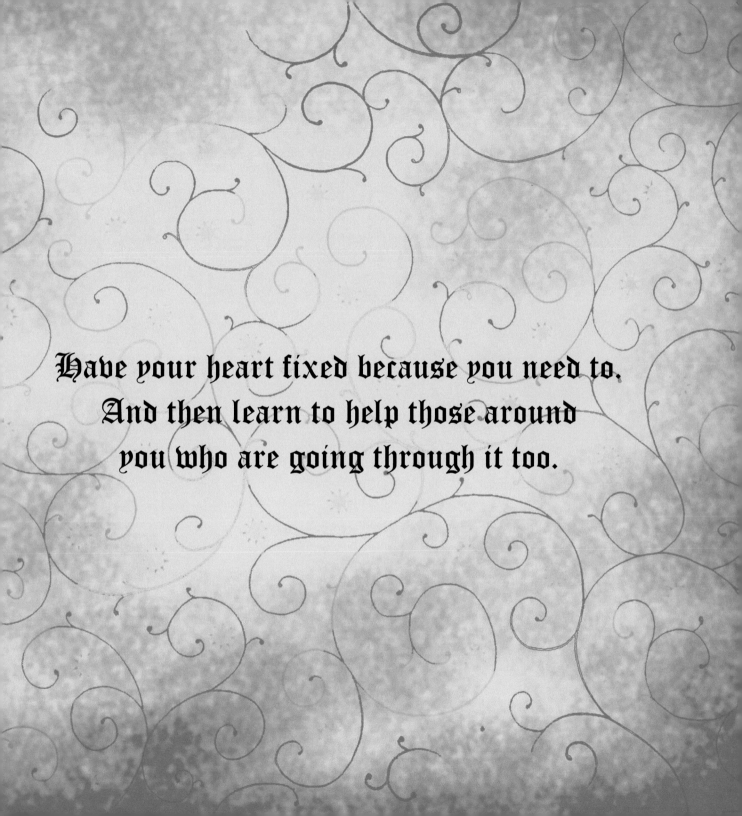

Have your heart fixed because you need to.
And then learn to help those around
you who are going through it too.

So off she went to the magical
place to get her heart fixed.
Not too long after, she leant to
her Mum who told her this;

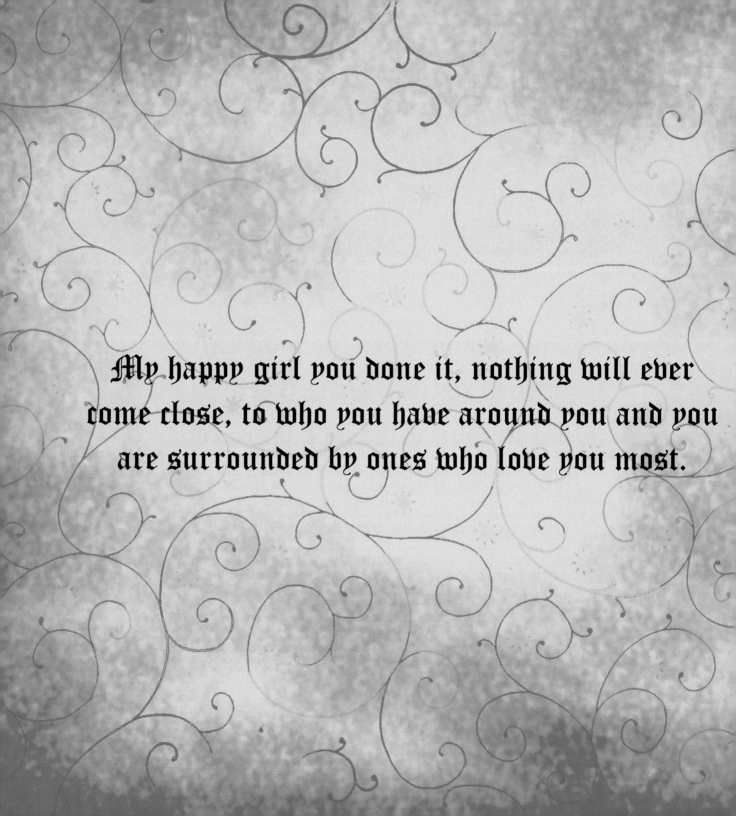

My happy girl you done it, nothing will ever come close, to who you have around you and you are surrounded by ones who love you most.

The Happy Heart Princess thanked
the fairies then went on her way,
Oh fairies there is just one thing
I would like to say -
Thank you for being as kind, as kind
can be, you done it with joy and love
and supported me endlessly.

Go spread your love happy princess
and if they do come to say
how did you princess get that
mark on your chest?
All you say is they only pick the best.
Now spread your love and pride with
that happy heart you hold inside.

The Happy Heart Princess went
to the place not too far away,
And spread her love equally
in each and every day.

She told people of her troubles and
how love got her through.
And told them to always spread
love in everything you do.

You never know who will need it,
they may need a happy heart.
Being kind and loving is the best place to start.
The Heart Princess smiled, and she's
smiling at you too as The Happy Heart
Princess will always be here for you.

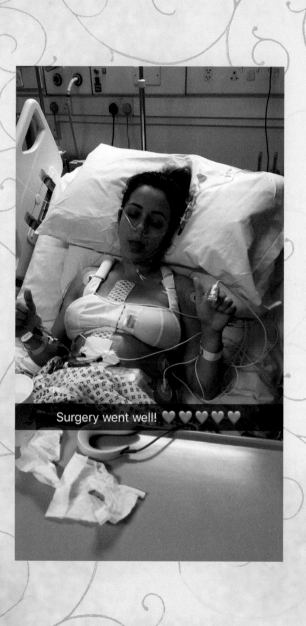

Surgery went well! 🤍🤍🤍🤍🤍

Leonie Jade Norton, 27, Hertfordshire. A story inspired by personal experience, hoping to help everyone effected by heart worries.

Printed in the United States
By Bookmasters